My Tooth Fell in

My Soup
and other poems

Erik Korhel

illustrated by Celia Marie Baker

Published by
Book Publishers Network
PO Box 2256
Bothell, WA 98041
425 483-3040
www.bookpublishersnetwork.com

ISBN10: 1-935359-02-9
ISBN13: 978-1-935359-02-9
LCCN: 2008940552

Book design: Celia Marie Baker

10 9 8 7 6 5 4 3 2 1

Dedication

There you were, Father,
As always when I was sick.

And you, Mother, on those days,
When I knew nothing else but to be sad.

Cheers! To the greatest team ever comprised.

My sister with me on those good days,
When we both were being bad.

To Be A Child

To be a child
Should I ever frown?

With everything so interesting
My small feet hardly touch the ground.

Love for all, this includes the sun and sky.
With only the most objectionable things
Will you ever see me cry.

Along with my imagination
How easy I make friends,
Where time doesn't exist
And the day never ends.

My smile never goes away.
I am happy just to catch a ball.
I ask myself, "What can't I do?"
"Nothing!" Because I can do it all!

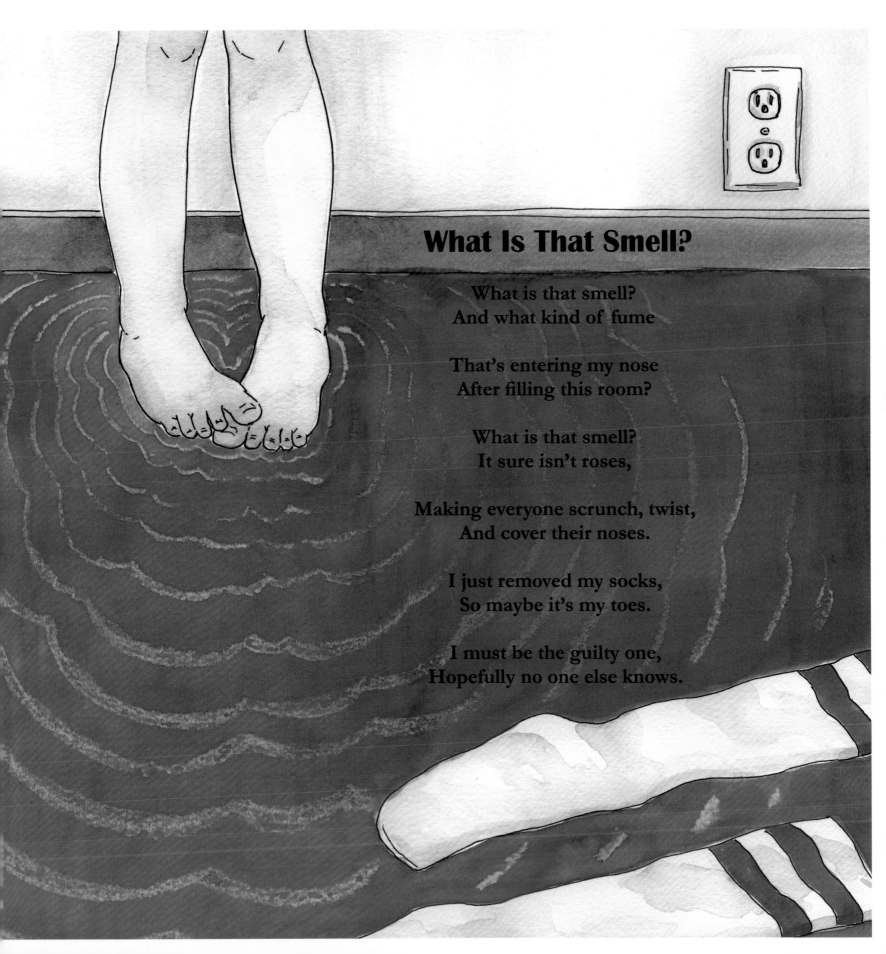

What Is That Smell?

What is that smell?
And what kind of fume

That's entering my nose
After filling this room?

What is that smell?
It sure isn't roses,

Making everyone scrunch, twist,
And cover their noses.

I just removed my socks,
So maybe it's my toes.

I must be the guilty one,
Hopefully no one else knows.

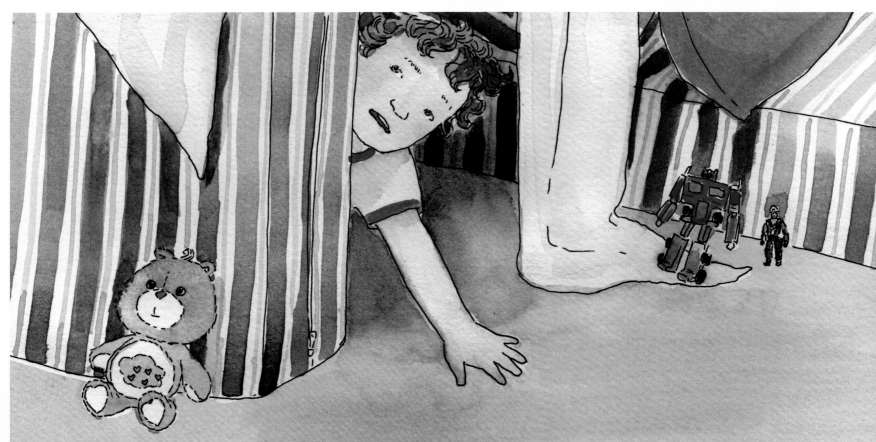

Wait Until I Tell Your Father

From the other room
I hear Mom ask me to stop.

"Not yet, Mom.
I'm seeing how long on one foot I can hop."

"I would like you to go play quietly in your room."

"I just removed all the cushions from the couch.
I am building a fort, but I'll be done soon."

"Out of the kitchen! You've already had your snack!"
"Oh, I wasn't taking this cookie. I was just putting it back."

"I am not going to tell you again.
Stop teasing your little sister!"

"That's not what I was doing at all.

"I was just giving her a big hug
And telling her how much I missed her."

"You need to go sit in the corner
Until the clock says fifteen minutes past."

"I am going to grab my favorite toy first.
That time always goes so slow, and I want it
to go fast."

Mom yells, "You haven't done a thing I've
asked
Or what you know you should!

"Just wait until I tell your father!"

"Ok, ok, I am sorry, Mom.
I promise now I will be good!"

Mud Puddle

I never met a mud puddle I didn't like,
Whether for making dirt pies
Or parting the center with my bike.

The puddle empties, becoming just another large hole
From the pouncing, stomping, and running about,
Though the heavy rain keeps quickly refilling it full
Like a faucet with a broken spout.

Now my shoes are soaked and toes a bit frozen.
Mom points and says,
"Straight to the hamper to drop those dirty clothes in!"

Saliva Napkin

Mom, please don't wipe my face
With your saliva napkin.

I don't ask much,
But this one thing I'm asking.

I am aware of the food
Around my mouth and mud on my cheeks.

I did wash my face,
Maybe not yesterday or today

But sometime within the last two weeks.

The Mailman Called Me
Little Girl

The mailman called me "little girl."
Is it the length of my hair
Or these tendril curls?

Embarrassed, I exclaim, "Hey, I'm a boy!"
And what next does he say?
"I wondered why a little girl would be dressed that way."

My Tooth Fell In My Soup

My tooth fell in my soup.

It wasn't the first where I noticed,
But on that second hearty scoop.

Must have dropped right out,
Apparently ready to fly the coop.

I didn't feel a splash
Or even hear it make a sound like "bloop."

Then again, I really wasn't expecting
My tooth to fall in to my soup.

Breathing Fire

"It's freezing outside!" Mom says.
"What have you been doing? Where have you been?"

"Outside inhaling and exhaling—
Pretending I'm a fire-breathing dragon."

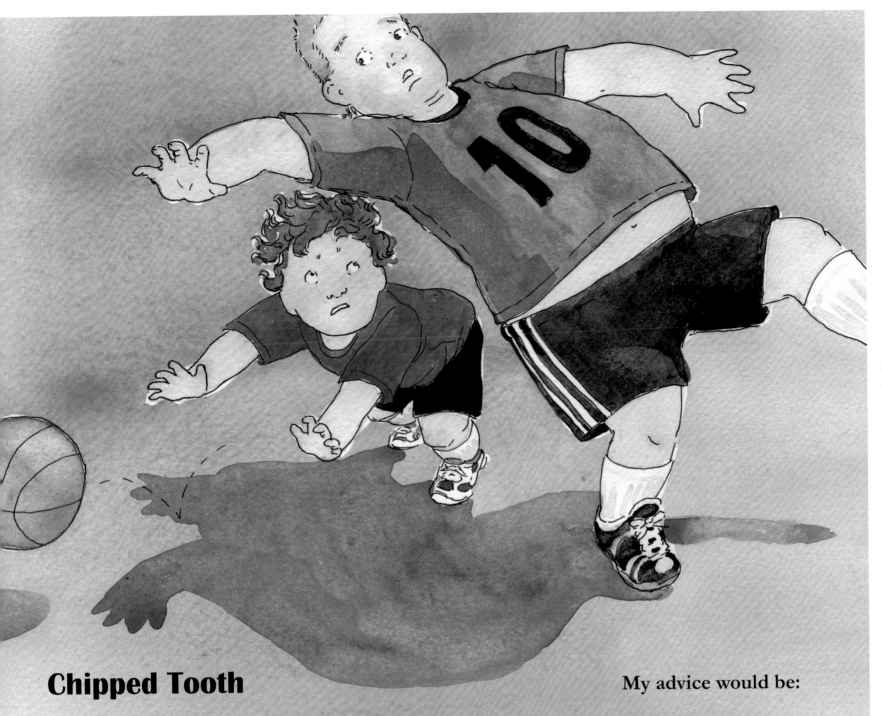

Chipped Tooth

My front tooth is chipped,
Now partially gone.

How did this happen?

A large boy fell on me,
His name is Ron.

My tooth is real sensitive,
Tingles with each scrape of
the tongue.

It wasn't all bad,
As the game we were playing
I eventually won.

My advice would be:

Now for a small boy,
You may find this a
challenge,

Try not to play with the
bigger boys
Who can't keep their balance.

Dark

After a nightmare,
I am still afraid, too.

What are those sounds I hear?
Mom, Dad, I hope that is you.

I can't roll over,
Still both frozen and scared.

I don't want to know what might be there.
And I refuse to do it, not even if dared.

If I pretend to still be asleep,
Here is what I believe.

If something is still lingering,
The sooner it becomes bored, the quicker
it will leave.

With the sun, hours from waking,
My imagination always does this in the
dark,

Left with my nightlight that offers a glow
Of no more than a tiny spark.

Finally the night is leaving,
And in comes the bright of the day.

Not that it really matters.
I wasn't afraid that whole time anyway.

Chewy???

"It appears as though you enjoy your food—
You chew and chew and chew.

"I have yet to see you swallow.
Is that mouthful almost through?

"Are you ok?
You don't look like you're choking.
Your face isn't turning blue.

"Please tell me what that is you're eating.
I am going crazy, ready to crawl the ceiling's beam!"

"Why, only the least chewy food I simply love to chew—
A giant, heaping bowl of vanilla ice cream."

Dinner

Is that what we are having for dinner?
But, Mom, you know I am so easy to please.
Wouldn't we all be much happier
With sliced hot dogs and macaroni and cheese?

Tonight I will just have dessert.
And out the window my dinner goes.
Mom won't even suspect a thing
As I will be the only one who knows.

I place everything properly in the sink.
"Yum, that was good,"
I let out with a hearty moan.
"Boy," Mom says, "you must have been hungry.
It seems you've even eaten the bone."

Saved by the sound of the doorbell ring
While at the same time my jaw just drops.
The neighbor is holding something at the door
and says,
"For dinner tonight, did you have pork chops?"

My Ears Are Burning

My ears are burning.
Now why could that be?
Is there someone,
Somewhere talking about me?

I hope it's only good things
And nothing too bad.
Well, I can't hear them anyway,
So there is no reason to get mad.

If only they would come
Just a little bit closer,
Maybe my ears wouldn't feel
Like they've been placed in a toaster.

Last Picked

Why does this keep happening?
I am always picked last.
Does that mean I am the worst
In my whole entire class?

How am I supposed to show you
And really give my all
When I am always sitting or leaning
As if I'm holding up this wall?

Who said they've seen me sleeping?
Who said they've heard me snore?
I guess always watching from the sidelines
Can be quite a bore.

Finally my turn to be team captain.
Does this mean I've been picked first?
Well, there is one thing I do know for sure:
This time I won't be considered the worst.

Sleepover

After a whole afternoon of trying,
My parents have finally let me
Stay the night at my best friend Ryan's.

Dad says, "If you're sure you want to,
But you know what often happens.
If you think you'll make it through."

"Whatever are you talking about?
We have a lot of fun planned,

Like eating everything in sight
While using only our hands.

"We're going to smash our toy cars,
Even have a pillow fight,
Causing such mischief at his house
That you are certain to hear about it
before the end of the night."

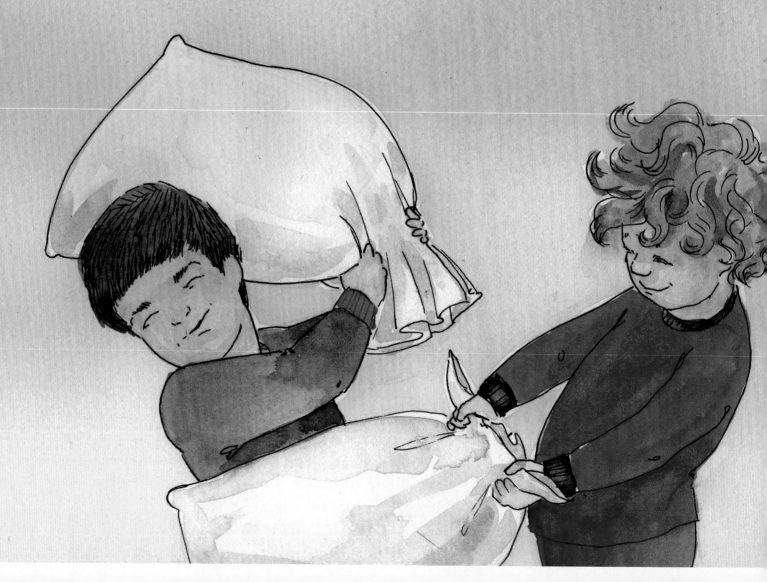

Now my eyes are getting sleepy.
I say goodnight to my parents on the phone.
This must have been what they were referring to earlier.
"Dad, could you please come get me?
I want to come home."

The Painter

I have orange in my
fingernails
And blue on my tips.
Yellow covers my shirt
While green covers my
hips.

I pick the perfect canvas.
It sits there white as snow.
I wonder, How do I
begin,
With a splatter, stroke, or
throw?

My palette is a rainbow.
My easel stands real tall.
I don't want to create just
one masterpiece,
So I will make them all.

First Love

As I sit, she caught me
Staring not once, but times three.
This angel who's name is Amanda
Is right here sitting next to me.

Her hair is short and blonde
With eyes that are glacier blue.
The teacher always catches us laughing.
"Ok, time to settle down, you two."

We often share our lunch,
Even trade our favorite dessert,
Wondering who will be the first of the day
To get it all over their shirt.

With enough courage, I wrote a note.
I'll give her after today's test.
It says, "Will you be my sweetheart?
Check a box, No, Maybe, or Yes."

Belt

"Where is the belt to my robe?" Dad says.
"I've been looking for an hour.

"If you've seen it, will you tell me?
I just want to take a shower.

"Why is it hanging from the back of your pajamas?
May I ask for one good answer?"

"Sure, I use your belt when I need a tail,
While make-believing I'm a panther."

The Lonely Phone

I am the lonely phone
With one bent bell.
Hearing me ring,
You can tell.

My cracked receiver
And rotary dial,
I am certainly a phone
Not seen in awhile.

Unable to hear a voice
On the other end of the line,
They'll say, "Speak a little
louder!
Are you able to hear mine?"

They pick me up,
Occasionally slam me down,

Toss me on the couch,
Grab me from the ground.

My cord gets tangled
From across the room
With back and forth paces.
To myself I think, "Please
be done soon."

They eat when they speak,
Leaving crumbs in my slots,
Whether potato chips or
crackers,
Crunch, crunch when they
talk.

I guess I am not so alone.
People talk and hold me,
Making me feel wanted and
needed.
Many times, they've told me.

Goodnight, Lovely

A warm glass of milk tops the rim.
A little snack, although just fed.
The clock hands tell me, won't be long
Before my bedtime story is read.

Time to put away my things
In a toy box big as a shed.
I'd better hurry; it's almost time
For my bedtime story to be read.

Chest of drawers opened top to bottom,
Finding pajamas no longer I dread.
Two arms in and two legs through,
I'm closer yet to a bedtime story being read.

Now late night arrives early.
"And I am not going to tell you again," Mommy said.
"Pick a book and warm the sheets.
Your bedtime story is about to be read."

I no longer say, "Just five more minutes,"
Seeing Mommy's face turn a beautiful gold to red.
Instead upstairs I go and brush my teeth.
Sooner is the bedtime story to be read.

The covers once straightened,
From the foot to the head,
Are swiftly pulled away.
A bedtime story's to be read.

The bookshelves are a shambles
As I climb into bed
From the excitement that is felt
Before my bedtime story is read.

The book cracks open, hearing a variety of voices,
Making sights and visions frolic in my head.
My eyes grow sleepy with something new.
Oh, the love of a bedtime story being read.

The End